Motocross™

Motocross Races

Janey Levy

PowerKiDS
press™

New York

To Tyrone, for his patience and for teaching me about motor sports

Published in 2007 by The Rosen Publishing Group, Inc.
29 East 21st Street, New York, NY 10010

First Edition

Editor: Joanne Randolph
Book Design: Ginny Chu
Layout Design: Kate Laczynski

Photo Credits: All photos © Simon Cudby Photo.

Library of Congress Cataloging-in-Publication Data

Levy, Janey.
  Motocross races / Janey Levy. — 1st ed.
      p. cm. — (Motocross)
  Includes index.
  ISBN-13: 978-1-4042-3696-7 (library binding)
  ISBN-10: 1-4042-3696-1 (library binding)
  1. Motocross—United States—Juvenile literature. 2. Motorcycles, Racing—United States—Juvenile literature. I. Title.
  GV1060.12.L48 2007b
  796.7'56—dc22
                                          2006032993

Manufactured in the United States of America

Contents

The Motocross Circuit

The motocross (MX), Supercross (SX), and Arenacross (AX) series are among the different types of immensely popular dirt-track motorcycle racing. Their tracks' twists, turns, hills, and jumps provide great excitement.

The American Motorcyclist Association (AMA) oversees these series. The AMA Motocross Championship is one series. The different races that make up the series occur on country courses with mostly natural features. The AMA Supercross Series takes place on large man-made courses in baseball or football stadiums. The AMA Arenacross Series occurs on smaller man-made courses in ice hockey and basketball arenas.

Freestyle MX (FMX or Moto-X) is motocross's newest form. In freestyle riders perform astounding tricks while flying through the air. The International Freestyle Motocross Association (IFMA) and the

Ricky Carmichael and James Stewart Jr. start the 2006 Southwick Motocross race side by side. It is often a battle to the finish for these two top riders.

World Freestyle Association (WFA) oversee freestyle events.

Women motocrossers have their own series. The Women's Motocross Association (WMA) oversees this series.

The AMA created the Motocross Championship series in 1972, 13 years after the earliest motocross event in the United States. Today the series is the top U.S. motocross series. It has 12 events in a season that runs from May to September. It begins and ends in California, the center of the motocross world. The season starts with the Hangtown Motocross Classic, in Sacramento. It ends with the Glen Helen National, in San Bernardino.

One of the stops on the AMA Motocross Championship series is at High Point Raceway, in Mount Morris, Pennsylvania. The High Point race is round two of the motocross season.

Racers roar through Glen Helen Raceway's huge Talladega Turn during the 2006 Glen Helen National.

The remaining 10 events are held at courses all over the country. Events occur in Pennsylvania, Massachusetts, Maryland, Michigan, New York, Colorado, Washington, and Minnesota. In addition to motocross races, the events include motocross lites races.

Riders come from around the world to take part in the series. They earn points based on how well they do at each event. The rider with the most points at the end of the season wins the championship.

The Motocross of Nations

The Motocross of Nations, also known by its French name, Motocross des Nations, takes place in Europe every year. It is the Olympics of motocross. Teams come from around the world to compete.

The AMA Supercross Series

The AMA Supercross Series began in 1976, with six events. Today the series has 16 events in a season that begins in January and ends in May. Supercross is enormously popular. More than 750,000 fans attend the events, and millions more watch them on television.

California is the center of the Supercross world, just as it is with motocross. Five of the 16 events take place in California. Three races are held in Anaheim, one in San Francisco, and one in San Diego. The AMA Supercross Series events also occur in Arizona, Missouri, Georgia, Indiana, Florida, Michigan, Texas,

Supercrossers get muddy during the 2006 AMA Supercross race in San Francisco, California.

The Anaheim track is being prepared for the first round of the 2006 AMA Supercross Series.

Washington, and Nevada. Just as motocross events include motocross lites, Supercross events include Supercross Lites.

Most of the same teams and riders take part in both the motocross and Supercross series. The two series combined have a total of 28 events. That is a lot of hard work for riders, teams, and machines!

Arenacross, like Supercross, takes place on man-made courses. However, since the courses are smaller than Supercross courses, with tighter twists and turns, the series draws a different group of riders. There

The U.S. Open of Supercross

The U.S. Open of Supercross has more prize money than any other motorcycle race. It is held every October in Las Vegas, Nevada. The first U.S. Open of Supercross was held in 1998.

Round two of the AMA Supercross Series takes place at Chase Field, in Phoenix, Arizona. Here riders are lined up for the start of the 2006 race.

are usually 14 events in the series. Arenacross makes a good winter sport, since it takes place indoors. The season begins in November and ends in February.

The Women's Motocross Series

Sarah Whitmore is shown here at the 2006 WMA Championship at Hangtown, in California. She finished in sixth place.

The first women's motocross championship was held in 1974. Nine thousand fans watched 300 women compete to become the Powder Puff National Champion. Not surprisingly women did not like that name. The next year the event was renamed the Women's Motocross Nationals.

Women had to work hard to gain support and establish a national series. Many people did not feel that women belonged in motocross. However, that view changed over time. Today the top women's motocross series is the AMA/WMA Pro Class Series. Talented riders come from around the world to compete in the

Jacqueline Ross started riding professionally in 2006. She has many amateur race wins under her belt, including wins in the 2004 and 2005 Mammoth Mountain Motocross events.

series. The WMA, which oversees the series, is a young organization. It was founded in 2004, after the leading women's motocross organization of the time, the Women's Motocross League (WML), stopped operating.

The Pro Class Series has six events in a season that begins in May and ends in September. The first two events are held in California. The remaining events are held in Colorado, Washington, New York, and Pennsylvania. Women also take part in Supercross and Arenacross.

The WMA Cup

The WMA Cup is the largest women's motocross race of the year. It has more prize money than any other women's race and more classes for amateurs. It is held in November every year.

Motocross at New York's Famous Unadilla Race Course

The AMA motocross course with the longest history is the one at the Unadilla Valley Sports Center, in New Berlin, New York. The center began holding professional motocross races in 1969, before the AMA Motocross Championship series had even been created. When the series was created in 1972, Unadilla was on the circuit. Over the next 20 years, AMA motocross events occurred at Unadilla off and on. Today the historic Unadilla course is a regular part of the circuit.

The first AMA championship event at Unadilla was held in 1972. The winner was Gary Jones. Damon Bradshaw won the first AMA motocross lites event at Unadilla in 1989. In 2006, superstar Ricky Carmichael won the motocross event. Rising star Ryan Villopoto won the motocross lites event.

Tim Ferry races in the 2006 Motocross Championship race at Unadilla. He finished the day in fifth place.

The Unadilla Valley Sports Center motocross track holds many races throughout the year for amateurs and professionals. Here riders tackle a hill in the 2006 Motocross Championship.

The Daytona Supercross

The Daytona Supercross is the most celebrated event on the American Supercross circuit. It takes place at Daytona International Speedway, a famous automobile racetrack in Daytona Beach, Florida. It began in the spring of 1971, when an AMA professional motocross event was staged on the field inside the racetrack. The event was moved to a more important and visible location in 1972. Some say that AMA Supercross started here, although the word "Supercross" was not invented until later in 1972.

Jim Weinert won the 1972 Daytona event. Ricky Carmichael won the 2006 Daytona Supercross, and David Millsaps won the 2006 Supercross Lites. Among the Daytona winners have been some of the greatest motocrossers of all time, including Roger DeCoster, Bob Hannah, and Jeremy McGrath.

You can see some of the man-made features on the Daytona Supercross track as fans make their way into the stadium for the 2006 Supercross Series event.

The X Games, originally called the Extreme Games, are the Olympics for extreme sports. Extreme sports include mountain biking, skateboarding, and, of course, motocross. Today the X Games include three motocross events. However, that was not always true.

A rider performs a Backflip Cordova in the 2006 X Games.

Motocross was not part of the first X Games, which took place in 1995. Freestyle MX was added in 1999. The next year the games added a step up competition. In step up riders race at high speeds up a ramp and attempt to leap over a bar that may

This rider has let go of his machine completely as he competes in the X Games. Tricks in which the rider does not touch the bike are some of the hardest to do.

be more than 30 feet (9 m) high! Then, in 2001, the X Games added big air, or best trick, which is a freestyle event. In best trick each rider performs the same trick three times, trying each time to be as perfect as possible.

Riders often show off new tricks at the X Games, and 2006 was no exception. Travis Pastrana performed a double backflip to win the best trick competition! Pastrana also won the freestyle MX event. Matt Buyten won the step up event.

Freestyle Series and Shows

The International Freestyle Motocross Association (IFMA) and the World Freestyle Association (WFA) each oversee a freestyle series. Groups of freestylers, such as the Metal Mulisha, also travel around the country putting on shows.

The Hangtown Motocross Classic

Riders make their way down a curving hill at Hangtown. Motocross races have been happening at this famous track for nearly 40 years.

The Hangtown Motocross Classic is the first AMA Motocross Championship event of the season. It takes its name from its original location, Placerville, California, which was once known as Hangtown. At the first event, the weather was bad, and only about 30 professional riders and 1,000 fans attended. However, the event kept growing. It was attracting more than 30,000 fans by

1979. That year it moved to the place where it is still held today, Prairie City State Vehicular Recreation Area, near Sacramento, California.

Today Hangtown is considered the series' senior, or highest-ranked, event. James Stewart Jr. won in 2006. The AMA/WMA Pro Class Series also holds an event in Hangtown each year. Jessica Patterson won in 2006.

The Glen Helen National

The final event of the AMA Motocross Championship series is the Glen Helen National. It takes place at Glen Helen Raceway, near San Bernardino, California. James Stewart Jr. won in 2006.

Races for Amateurs

There are also plenty of events for amateurs. Here are four of the biggest ones.

Riders bunch together toward the beginning of this amateur championship race at Loretta Lynn's ranch. The pack will start to break up as the race goes on.

The National Motorsports Association (NMA) oversees the World Mini Grand Prix, which began in 1972. It takes place every year at Las Vegas Motor Speedway, in Nevada. Riders from all over the United States and the world compete here.

The NMA also oversees the Grand National Motocross Championships. This event began in 1976 and takes place in Ponca City, Oklahoma.

The AMA oversees the Winter National Olympics, also known as the Mini Olympics or Mini O's. They began in 1972 and take place at Gatorback Cycle Park, near Gainesville, Florida. The Mini O's include both motocross and Supercross events.

The biggest amateur event is the AMA Amateur National Motocross Championships, which began in 1982. It takes place at country singer Loretta Lynn's ranch in Tennessee. Superstars Jeremy McGrath, Ricky Carmichael, Travis Pastrana, and James Stewart Jr. all won here.

Loretta Lynn's ranch is a great course with lots of natural curves, hills, and jumps.

Here riders round a corner during the 2006 AMA Amateur National Championships.

If you are an amateur who wants to reach the top, practice and compete as much as possible. Then one day you may get to compete in one of these big events!

Some Famous Firsts

- **Winner of the first-ever race in the AMA Motocross Championship series:** Sonny DeFeo (1972)
- **Winner of the first AMA Motocross Championship:** Gary Jones (1972)
- **Winner of the first AMA Motocross Lites Championship:** Marty Smith (1974)
- **Winner of the first women's motocross championship (Powder Puff Grand National Champion):** Nancy Payne (1974)
- **Winner of the first AMA Supercross Series championship:** Jim Weinert (1976)
- **Winner of the first AMA Arenacross championship:** Dennis Hawthorne (1986)
- **Winner of the first U.S. Open of Supercross:** Damon Huffman (1998)
- **Winner of the first X Games freestyle competition:** Travis Pastrana (1999)
- **Winner of the first X Games step up competition:** Tommy Clowers (2000)
- **Winner of the first X Games big air (best trick) competition:** Kenny Bartman (2001)

Glossary

amateurs (A-muh-turz) People who do something as a hobby, for free.

arenas (uh-REE-nuz) Small stadiums inside buildings.

backflip (BAK-flip) A trick in which the rider and machine flip backward while flying through the air, spin completely around, and land right side up.

extreme (ik-STREEM) Going past the expected or common.

grand prix (GRAHN PREE) A high-level event in a sport such as racing.

historic (hih-STOR-ik) Famous or important in history.

motocross lites (MOH-toh-kros LYTS) A motocross series for machines with engines half the size of regular motocross machines.

professional (pruh-FESH-nul) Someone who is paid for what he or she does.

ramp (RAMP) A sloping platform.

ranch (RANCH) A large farm for raising cows, horses, or sheep.

recreation (reh-kree-AY-shun) A hobby, or something done for fun.

speedway (SPEED-way) A racecourse for automobiles or motorcycles.

stadiums (STAY-dee-umz) Large buildings for sports events surrounded by rising rows of seats for fans. A stadium usually does not have a roof.

Supercross Lites (SOO-per-kros LYTS) A Supercross series for machines with engines half the size of regular Supercross machines.

vehicular (vee-HIH-kyuh-lur) Having to do with motor vehicles, such as cars, motorcycles, or ATVs.

Index

Web Sites

Due to the changing nature of Internet links, PowerKids Press has developed an online list of Web sites related to the subject of this book. This site is updated regularly. Please use this link to access the list:

www.powerkidslinks.com/motoc/races/